Captain No Be...

AN IMAGINARY TALE OF A PIRATE'S LIFE

Carole P. Roman

For Alexander,
Who reminded me how much fun
it was to go from the bottom of the sea
to the most distant star. All in one day!

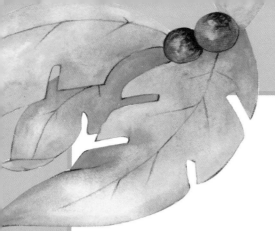

Captain No Beard lived on a small island with his hearty bunch of mates. There was Mongo the mast-climbing monkey, Linus the loud-mouthed lion, Fribbit the floppy frog, and of course Hallie, his first mate and cousin.

They sailed on his mighty frigate, the *Flying Dragon*. Captain No Beard chose that name because it sounded scary.

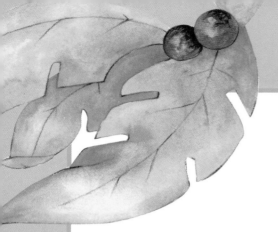

Every morning Captain No Beard
gathered his crew and gave
out the orders of the day.
"Swab the decks, pump the bilges,
climb the mast, and shiver me timbers!"

"'Shiver me timbers?'" Hallie asked.
"What does that mean?"
Captain No Beard thought and thought.
"A good first mate knows the
answers!" he declared.
"But how will I know if you don't
tell me?" Hallie asked.

Captain No Beard pulled out his handy Pirate Dictionary and scanned the pages. "Hmm…let me see." He scratched thoughtfully at his smooth chin. "'Shiver me timbers'… 'shiver me timbers'… aha! It says right here that 'shiver me timbers' means 'oh my goodness!' in Pirate." "Argh! Argh!" the crew shouted in approval. "Shiver me timbers!"

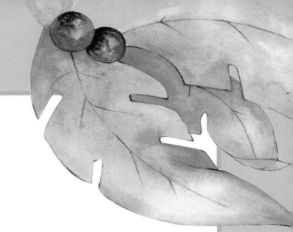

They ran off to swab the decks, pump the bilges, and climb the mast, all the while crying, "Shiver me timbers!" Captain No Beard sighed. "Being a captain is hard work."

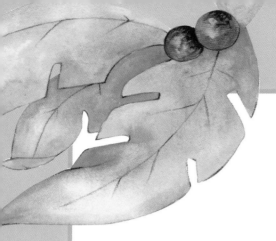

Mongo climbed the mainmast
and scanned the horizon.
"Sail ho!" He pointed south.

Captain No Beard looked through his spyglass. Sure enough, there was a big fluffy white thing in the distance, but it was a cloud, not a ship.

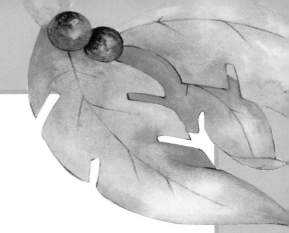

"Mongo," he called back, "there is no ship yonder. A storm is brewing!"

Clouds started to roll in. Fribbit the frog flopped over to the captain. "Aye Captain, I think we're in for a big blow."
Captain No Beard looked at the rumbling sky and grey waves lapping the sides of the ship.
"Aye, me hearties, I think you're right. Sound the alarm!"
"Sound the alarm!" Fribbit yelled to Linus.

Linus used his best, loudest roar.
"All hands on deck! All hands on deck!
Batten down the hatches!"
Hallie, Linus, Fribbit, and Mongo ran to
their posts to tie down the equipment.

Captain No Beard sighed.
"Being a captain is hard work."

Soon the ship was rocking to and fro. "Hold on, mateys!" Captain No Beard yelled.

The *Flying Dragon* tilted and swayed on the stormy sea. Hallie lost her grip and starting rolling towards the edge of the deck. "Help!" she cried.

Fribbit sounded the alarm. "Man—I mean girl—I mean first mate overboard! I mean almost overboard!"

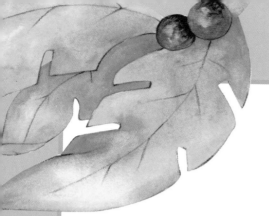

Captain No Beard inched toward her.
The rain beat down, thunder boomed,
lightning flashed.
The captain stretched as far as
he could and grabbed Hallie's hand,
pulling her to safety.

"Whew, that was close,"
Captain No Beard said.
"Being a captain is hard work."

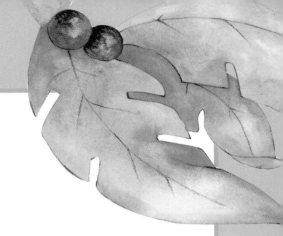

The sun peeked through the clouds and the sea calmed. It was time to swab the decks again.

"What's going on up there?"
a voice called from the deep, dark sea.
Everyone stopped.
"Who goes there?" Captain No Beard
asked cautiously.
The voice seemed to come all the way
from Davy Jones's Locker.
"I said, what's going on up there?"
The crew all looked at each other.
"Shiver me timbers!" they whimpered.

Brave Hallie whispered, "It's a mermaid!"
"How do you know that?" the captain asked.
"Good first mates know
all the answers, remember?"
"Oh. Right," the captain said.
"What are we going to do?"
They huddled together.

Captain No Beard thought and thought.
The crew looked to him for answers.
"Being a captain is hard work," he sighed.
At last he spoke up in his best pirate voice.
"We be lookin' for treasure, mermaid.
Do you have any? Argh!"

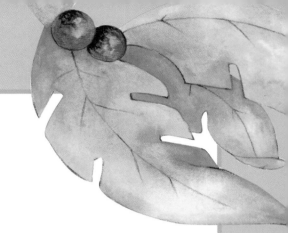

He heard soft laughter, which grew louder and louder. The crew edged closer and closer to him. Suddenly, there on the starboard bow of the *Flying Dragon*, was the mermaid herself!

"Why are the lights off? Look at this mess! Your bed is a disaster, Alexander! You'll have to clean all this up before dinner." Then the mermaid looked at the crew and smiled. "Did I hear you say you were looking for treasure?" She lowered a plate filled with golden cookies. "I come bearing doubloons. Just don't leave any crumbs, me hearties." The pirates all bellowed, "Argh! Argh! Argh!"

With that the mermaid winked,
left the plate of treasure, and
disappeared back into the sea.
Captain No Beard and all the crew
sat down for a pirate feast.
"Have another cookie, Captain," Hallie said.
"I'm too full," the captain groaned, patting
his belly. "Being a captain is hard work."

Made in the USA
San Bernardino, CA
10 September 2013